SPORTSMANSHIP

Sometimes, the desire to win gets in the way of good sportsmanship.

THE VALUES LIBRARY

SPORTSMANSHIP

John S. Bowman

THE ROSEN PUBLISHING GROUP, INC.
NEW YORK

Published in 1990 by The Rosen Publishing Group, Inc.
29 East 21st Street, New York, NY 10010.

First Edition
Copyright 1990 by The Rosen Publishing Group, Inc.

Printed in Canada
Bound in the United States of America

Library of Congress Cataloging-in-Publication Data

Bowman, John.
    Sportsmanship / John Bowman.
    (The Values library)
    Includes bibliographical references.
    Index.
    Summary: Examines the differences between good and bad
sportsmanship.
    ISBN 0-8239-1110-1
    1. Sportsmanship—Juvenile literature.   [1. Sportsmanship.]
I. Title.   II. Series.
GV708.3.B69   1990   89-70127
175—dc20   CIP
                                                      AC

CONTENTS

DO YOU KNOW IT WHEN YOU SEE IT?

EVERYONE HAS HEARD OF GOOD SPORTSMANSHIP and poor sportsmanship. Maybe you can't describe them. But you know the difference between them.

The whole world enjoyed a picture from the 1988 Olympics. Al Joyner was spinning his wife Florence around. She had just set a world record in the 200 meter race. Al Joyner had failed to make the U.S. Olympic team. But he had helped coach his wife to victory. That's good sportsmanship.

Another revealing photograph was taken at the 1989 Mets spring training camp. It shows Darryl Strawberry and Keith Hernandez fighting during a team photo session. That's poor sportsmanship.

Can we always tell good sportsmanship from bad? Is it
always so obvious? Think about situations like these.

The hard-fought basketball game is down to the final
22 seconds. Illinois is leading Syracuse by only 3 points.
Syracuse has called for a "time-out." The TV sportscaster
makes a casual remark. "Well, this game is going to be
played with fouls from here on." He is correct. In those
final seconds, Syracuse players foul Illinois players time
after time. Yet the referees don't call for any special penalties. The crowds cheer madly. Viewers around the
country admire the Syracuse team. They fail to beat
Illinois, but no one accuses them of bad sportsmanship.

In the 1984 Olympics, Carl Lewis was expected to win
four gold medals. Fans hoped he would set new world
records. On his first attempt in the long jump, Lewis did
very well. He decided not to try again unless another
jumper did better. No one did, so Lewis won the event.
But he had not tried to set a new world record. Later,
Lewis explained his action. He said he wanted to save his
energy. He wanted to do well in his other events. Some
people thought Carl Lewis showed poor sportsmanship.
To those people good sportsmanship means always trying
your hardest, no matter what.

People see sportsmanship in different ways. Fouls are
sometimes fair. Champions are sometimes booed. Like

many things in this world, sportsmanship is not a simple thing.

You may be saying, "I'm not an athlete. I don't even care about team games. I don't need to worry about sportsmanship." But is sportsmanship only about sports?

True, the word "sports" is part of sportsmanship. But does that mean sportsmanship concerns only athletes? Is good or poor sportsmanship displayed only in sporting contests? That is a question this book will try to answer.

Notice the word "man" in "sportsmanship." When the word came into being, almost all athletes were male. Today, of course, females of all ages are active in sports of all kinds. So sportsmanship is something for everyone to think about.

Learning to understand sportsmanship can be interesting. It can help you see your own values and priorities. Priorities are what you place first in your life. Values are ideals and goals that are important to the way you live. When you understand sportsmanship, you can discover some things about yourself.

There are many ways to think about an idea we want to understand. One way is to look up its meaning in the dictionary. Try that with "sportsmanship." You will see something like this:

> *conduct that involves fair and honest rivalry, courteous relations, and graceful acceptance of the results.*

That sounds simple enough. That sounds reasonable.
But is it that easy to see in real life?

Does your school have strong rivalries with teams from
other schools? Most schools do. Winning these contests
is important. The teams, the coaches, and the fans get
very excited. Perhaps the athletes push and shove just a
bit harder than usual in such a game. Perhaps the
coaches get a bit louder than usual. Perhaps the referees
do make a few mistakes. Supporters of both teams get
very involved in the game. The situation can get unpleas-
ant, even ugly. A friendly rivalry can end in harsh words,
or even swinging fists.

What happens? Where does good sportsmanship end
and poor sportsmanship begin? Dictionary definitions are
exact. In our everyday life, things are not always that
clear. Sometimes the difference between good and poor
sportsmanship isn't easy to see.

Team spirit and a competitive attitude are part of school life.

1

MODERN PRESSURES

IN OUR MODERN WORLD, new pressures make it harder to live up to the ideals of sportsmanship.

For example, today many people blindly admire athletes. You don't have to turn on a television set to see this. Look around your own school. Who are the most admired young people? Are they the editors of the school newspaper? Are they the officers of the drama club? No, they are probably the athletes. This is also true on many college campuses. And the popularity of sports stars around the world is greater than ever before.

The interest in athletes and sports in our society starts at a very early age. Younger and younger kids are expected to take part in organized sports. These young players must have uniforms and all the other "official" gear. There are cheerleaders at junior high games now. Many communities support youth teams with all kinds of "booster" clubs and fund drives. Parents become very involved in their children's success at sports. Coaches feel they must produce winners. All this puts a lot of pressure on the kids.

11

It doesn't have to lead to poor sportsmanship. It doesn't always. But it can. It is not good to make kids feel that winning is everything. The losers feel crushed. The winners feel like superstars. All because one youth team beat another, 5-2.

There used to be a tradition in sports that winners never boasted in public. They never bragged in front of their opponents. A winner was expected to say something like, "We had a bit of luck, I guess. The other team played really well, too."

Now that has changed. Even before the game is over, the team that seems sure to win start wagging their fingers. By the time the team wins, the players are publicly boasting. "We're Number One," they shout.   You'd think they just won the Super Bowl. What they mean is that their football team beat the team from the neighboring school.

Much of this "Number One" boasting is brought on by television. And it is usually done in good spirits. But it is a new version of good sportsmanship. In the past, players let other people say they were good athletes. No player claimed to be better than the others. Some of those old ways are worth bringing back.

Some of the old ways do still live. After many youth games and school sports contests, members of the teams

"High fives" are a way to inspire a winning attitude.

give their opponents a "high five." Some schools still
keep up another old habit: The winners get in a huddle
and cheer the losing team. Perhaps that isn't necessarily

proof of better sportsmanship. But some of those old-fashioned ways do seem to create a more friendly contest. You might consider getting your teammates to try this. Especially if you find the fun has gone out of the game.

There are other pressures on sports players today. Most people train very hard. It takes work to get ahead in sports. This is also true in many other areas of life. Education is training. Taking courses in computers is training. That is what getting ahead in life is all about. There is nothing against the law or unsportsmanlike about being well prepared and very determined. But it does lead to a very high level of competition.

The modern Olympic Games are a good example. They were started in 1896 to promote good will between countries and amateur (a-mah-tuhr) sports. Today the Games are used to stir feelings of love of country. Young athletes are not just competing for the fun of it. They are made to feel that they must win for the glory of their country. If they don't win a medal, they feel that they have let their country down.

It is hard for athletes today to keep old-fashioned sportsmanship. Modern sports can put a lot of pressure on young people. Some young people may get the wrong idea. They might think that anything goes, as long as it leads to winning. Young people today have to be very strong to stand up to these pressures.

2

ON THE SIDELINES

YOUNG PEOPLE TODAY MAY HAVE TROUBLE learning good sportsmanship. There is a reason for this problem. Adults do not always provide the best examples of sportsmanship.

Look at some of the coaches of teams in recent years. Bobby Knight of basketball, Woody Hayes of football, and Billy Martin of baseball are examples. They may be admired for their winning teams. But their personal behavior is often not very admirable. Some of these coaches throw fits, others throw chairs. Sometimes they themselves are thrown out.

Television allows everyone to see if not hear the foul language some coaches use. Some coaches' behavior is so extreme that it is laughable. But these coaches offer young people very poor examples of sportsmanship.

One example was provided in the winter basketball season of 1989. We will not name the coach. His hometown fans were unhappy with some of the referees' calls. They were throwing things onto the court. A referee told the coach to ask his fans to stop. Otherwise their team would have to forfeit the game. The coach agreed. He

15

took the mike and said, "In spite of the bad refereeing, you must stop throwing things." It makes an amusing story. But is this the way to teach good sportsmanship? That coach set a bad example for the team and the fans.

Adults at many colleges and universities set another example of poor sportsmanship. Coaches, athletic department officials, administrators, even teachers are guilty. They break many rules trying to build their school teams. Sometimes these adults pay money to recruit players. That is illegal. Then they continue to pay the players. They pretend the players work at salaried jobs at school. Many athletes can take easy courses. Sometimes passing grades are given to players for little or no work. These things have no place in school sports. They are the very opposite of the values of honesty and integrity.

In fact, these practices do not have much to do with sportsmanship. Many of these college athletes are dropped if they are not high scorers. At some schools winning is more important than learning. Most of the young men in Division I college basketball never graduate. These young athletes are being used by the coaches and colleges that recruit them. They find out that people they trusted never cared about them. These athletes have risked their future in sports and in life.

Coaches and college officials are not the only prob-

Fans can often demonstrate poor sportsmanship.

lems. The parents of young athletes often show poor sportsmanship. Some parents put pressure on their kids to be the best. To try for excellence is fine. But *always* to win? To be *only* the best? Not all children can possibly live up to such goals.

Many kids just like to "play the game." They have the true amateur spirit. Some parents burn out this light of pleasure in the game.

Some families and friends who come to team games become too excited. Sometimes parents embarrass their children on the court or field. They shout out loud to their kids during the game. Most children get upset when that happens.

Sportsmanship is often the poorest when a child's team is losing. Parents may become especially upset about anything that goes wrong. Suddenly an umpire turns into a blind dummy. It would be funny if it weren't so embarrassing. These parents are not setting an example of good sportsmanship.

Fans of all kinds can be terrible models for young people. Of course, everyone wants their side to win. But there should be some limit to how we show our support. We can be positive about our side without being negative about the other team. You can boo and jeer in fun. Everyone knows that this is part of a game. But nasty booing and jeering is very poor sportsmanship.

Sometimes fans decide they don't like one athlete. These people boo and jeer whenever that athlete appears on the field. A few baseball players are treated this way every season.

Ted Williams was one of the greatest hitters of all time. But when he played for the Boston Red Sox he was often booed. Williams was able to take it, but not all athletes are that strong.

One of the saddest cases was Roger Maris. He was never as popular as his Yankee teammate, Mickey Mantle. The 1961 season was very exciting. Mantle and Maris were both closing in on Babe Ruth's record. Ruth had hit 60 home runs in one season. If the record had to be broken, most people wanted Mickey to do it. He stalled at 54. Maris went on to hit number 61 on the last day of the season. Baseball fans all over the country turned against Maris. They booed him when he came to bat. And they shouted nasty things at him when he was out in the field.

Finally Maris asked to be traded from the Yankees. He spent his final playing years with the St. Louis Cardinals. Roger Maris was a serious professional athlete. But those nasty fans spoiled his enjoyment of the game.

Next time you are about to boo or jeer at an athlete, stop and think. Don't criticize or make fun of someone who is trying hard to do their best. Have you earned the right to be so mean?

As strange as it may sound, don't always follow the examples of adults around you. They may be showing poor sportsmanship. As you grow older, you will be able to tell the difference. Maybe you can't correct or criticize adults. But you can certainly go your own way. You can be a good sportsman on your own. And you can promise yourself you won't act in such unsportsmanlike ways.

The coach should set the example for sportsmanlike conduct both on and off the field.

3

A TALE OF THREE COACHES

WHY DO SO MANY PEOPLE BELIEVE that winning at games is so important? Maybe the answer is in the stories of three famous American athletic coaches.

The first is no longer well known. T.A.D. Jones was the coach of Yale's football team between 1916 and 1927. Yale's biggest rival was Harvard College. One year, before that game, Jones talked to his team: "Gentlemen, you are about to play Harvard. Never again will you do anything as important."

That showed the team members that they were expected to play their best game. And they probably did. But the coach did not say anything about winning. He said that playing in such a game was important. Win or lose, what mattered was to give it your best effort.

That is the original spirit of amateur athletics: Playing The Game Is What Counts. This was the spirit in school sports and amateur athletics during the first half of the 20th century. Many professional contests were also based on it.

Little League baseball should teach kids how to lose as well as how to win.

Chapter Three

Vince Lombardi, famous coach of the Green Bay Packers, was known for his intensity and dedication to winning.

About 1950, that began to change. There were many causes. Sports became more professional and more money was riding on sporting events. Teams had to become more competitive. Athletes had to be more serious. That changed the spirit behind sports contests. The new spirit was shown in the words of another famous coach, Vince Lombardi.

Lombardi's name is still well known. The trophy named after him is given each year to the best college lineman. Between 1959 and 1968, Lombardi coached the Green Bay Packers, a professional football team. During those years Lombardi led the Packers to five NFL titles and two Super Bowl wins. Lombardi was known for his total dedication. And he expected his players to make a 110 percent effort in every game. Coach Lombardi once said, "Winning isn't everything. It's the only thing."

These words show the attitude of many people today, in sports and in other parts of life. It is no longer enough just to play. It is no longer enough to do your best. It is no longer enough to want to win or to try to win. You *must* win! Nothing else counts.

This attitude can be seen most clearly among the many coaches who use Vince Lombardi as their model. They are intense, dedicated, demanding. You can see these coaches on TV. You may even have this kind of coach at your school.

Not everyone agrees with this approach to sports, especially for young people. This is their right. But let us be fair. Does this way of thinking have to rule out good sportsmanship? Does a "winning is everything" idea have to lead to poor sportsmanship?

In fact, it doesn't. No one ever accused Vince Lombardi of telling his players to "play dirty." No one ever

said his Green Bay Packers broke the rules. There is no
reason why wanting to win means the end of good
sportsmanship. You should be able to play hard and still
play fair and square.

In real life, though, things may be a little harder.
When there is a great need to win, there may be more
temptation to try to cheat.

Another famous coach believed that "anything goes, as
long as you win." Leo "The Lip" Durocher played short-
stop from 1925 to 1945. He was best known, however, as
the manager of the Brooklyn Dodgers and New York
Giants in the 1940s and 1950s. As his nickname suggests,
Durocher was a colorful character. He was famous for his
hot temper and sharp language. He was always tough.
He was known for being a not-so-nice guy. Once, when
someone remarked about this, Durocher supposedly
snarled, "Nice guys finish last!"

Anyone can adopt Durocher's words as their personal
slogan. But that says more about them than about what
goes on in the world.

Durocher's remark should not be confused with
Lombardi's remark. You can be a "nice guy" and still be
totally set on winning. Playing to win doesn't have to
do away with good sportsmanship. Neither does working
hard to be the best.

4

DRUGS AND SPORTS DON'T MIX

A Special Case

There is a new thing in sports that breaks with the idea of sportsmanship. It is usually illegal, often dangerous, and sometimes deadly. Unfortunately some people accept it. This new thing is drug use.

At first, drugs may seem to have nothing to do with sportsmanship, good or bad. But drugs have entered every part of our lives, including athletics. Drugs force us to think again about what we mean by sportsmanship.

There are two kinds of drugs that threaten to destroy sports and athletes. One type includes those dangerous things called "recreational" drugs. These are not medicine. These are chemicals that people use to relax and to have a good time. Such drugs are not known to help athletes. Indeed, they would probably hurt their performance.

Drugs and sports do not mix.

The most common of these drugs is widely accepted in our society. Most people believe adults can drink alcoholic beverages in moderation without harm. Adult athletes can handle a reasonable amount of alcohol in their off hours and still perform well. Alcohol, particularly beer, is promoted in advertising as though it has a special role in athletes' lives.

The plain fact is that young people under 21 are forbidden by law to drink alcohol. It is also a fact that many young people break this law. However, they should think very carefully before starting to drink. This is especially true if they intend to engage in sports. Even if drinking is limited to weekends or special parties, alcohol makes a young body pay a price. Too much alcohol can be just plain dangerous, to others and to oneself.

Besides alcohol, well-known recreational drugs include marijuana, cocaine, crack, LSD, and amphetamines. Many young people have died from the overuse or abuse of these drugs. They may have started out thinking they could handle them. But soon the drugs were stronger than they were. The victims of these drugs include young people from all walks of life. Athletes seem to be the best known cases.

One of the saddest cases involving an athlete was that of Len Bias. He was a 22-year-old basketball star for the

Len Bias died from an overdose of cocaine. He had just signed to play basketball for the Boston Celtics.

University of Maryland. In 1986, he was the first pick of the Boston Celtics. Len Bias's whole life was about to open up. He would have a career in the NBA and a huge salary.

On the first night after he signed his contract, he went to a party. There he "sniffed" too much cocaine. Within hours, his heart stopped and he was dead. Len Bias was not a drug addict. He had used cocaine on only a few "social" occasions. Yet this one mistake cost him his life.

Such a story, of course, goes beyond sportsmanship. It is a tragic tale. But the use and abuse of recreational drugs does often affect sports. Many well known athletes

in various sports have admitted using cocaine and other drugs. Some have gone to jail. Others have lost their careers in organized sports. Many other athletes, such as Dwight Gooden, have caught themselves in time. They have gotten help and kicked a drug habit.

The fact is that using "recreational" drugs is illegal. Athletes who use drugs are breaking the law. Athletes can sometimes hide their habits from teammates and fans. But most begin to slip in their performance. At that point, they are not only breaking the law. They are breaking the code of good sportsmanship.

This is an important part of sportsmanship. As a team member, the way you act affects the lives of other people. Recreational drugs are illegal. Your use of drugs can affect the success of your team. If that happens, it becomes a matter of sportsmanship.

The Performance Enhancers

Another kind of drugs affect athletic performances directly. These are "enhancement" or stimulant drugs. They are taken to gain advantages in competition. Athletes hope for greater strength, greater endurance, greater bursts of energy.

In recent years, one particular drug has swept through the sports world: anabolic steroids. These drugs are

All Olympic athletes must be tested for illegal substances.

made of the same chemicals found in the male hormone, testosterone. Anabolic steroids are supposed to make people super-performers. They build up size and strength, quickly and easily.

Many athletes find that they can increase their performances if they use anabolic steroids. The effects can be continued for several years. Weightlifters have used anabolic steroids. Bodybuilders, football players, and track and field athletes (runners, high-jumpers, and such) use them, too. Many athletes in all kinds of sports use them. There are rumors that some baseball players use steroids.

Anabolic steroids are a prescription drug. They are very powerful. They can be very dangerous. Most of the athletes using them are breaking the law. They are using these drugs without a doctor's prescription. They are breaking the rules of good sportsmanship. What they are doing is dangerous and illegal. Most major athletic groups have ruled that athletes may not use steroids. So the users are breaking those rules, too. And they are cheating on their fellow competitors. They are trying to gain an advantage with illegal drugs.

The price young athletes pay for the temporary advantage of steroid use can be terrible. At least one young person has died. He was a high school student in Ohio. He wanted to be bigger and stronger. He wanted to play on the school football team. He wanted to impress the girls. He took anabolic steroids to build up his slight body. No one knows if the girls were impressed. But he did make the team. And he played well. After an important football game of the 1988 season, he was named "player of the game." Three days later, he was dead. The exact cause could not be pinned down. But his death was almost certainly due to his use of anabolic steroids.

Some weight lifters use anabolic steroids to improve performance and create large muscles.

Many other young men have suffered serious side effects. Some of these are physical. Anabolic steroids can damage the liver and kidneys. They can cause high blood pressure. They may decrease a man's sperm count. They can make a man unable to have sex. Women who take steroids have problems with their menstrual periods. They can become more masculine-looking. Other effects of steroids can make people very violent and aggressive. Users can have problems controlling their tempers.

One young football player came forward in 1988. He told his story in the pages of *Sports Illustrated* magazine. The coach and trainers of his college football team encouraged him to take anabolic steroids. They said he would become a stronger player. He did become stronger—but he also went almost insane. He began to do stranger and stranger things. He picked fights, smashed metal objects, even threatened other people with weapons.

Things got so bad that the young man considered killing himself. Fortunately, he went for help before he did any serious harm to others or to himself. What happened to him is an example of what anabolic steroids can do. They can break down your mind while building up your muscles.

This young athlete is very bitter about what happened to him. His team's coaches saw how the steroids had affected him. But they simply ignored the problem. They acted as though they didn't care about him at all. This raises an important question. Who showed the worst sportsmanship in this case? The young man's coaches behaved very badly. They only cared about having a winning team.

Is there anything good to say for taking drugs? Are there any other sides to this terrible story?

Maybe there are a few confusing lines where drugs are concerned. Caffeine, nicotine, and alcohol are obviously accepted by our society. Athletes with health problems may be allowed to take special medicines. But the lines between sportsmanship and illegal drugs are clear. Drugs have no place in the lives of any young people, athletes or not. This lack of sportsmanship is also self-defeating.

"Shoeless Joe" Jackson was one of the 1919 Chicago White Sox accused of "throwing" the World Series.

5

OUT OF BOUNDS

THE LINE BETWEEN GOOD AND BAD SPORTSMANSHIP may not always be easy to see. But that doesn't mean that anything goes. Some actions on a court or playing field are just plain unacceptable. Some are just plain illegal.

Any action that is illegal is clearly outside the bounds of sportsmanship. Hunters who "jack" animals, for instance, are worse than just poor sports. "Jacking" refers to shining bright lights into the eyes of animals at night. Many animals remain still in the light. Hunters can easily shoot them. This is illegal. It is also illegal to kill more than a certain number of animals. It is illegal to catch more than a certain number of fish. These limits are set to protect the numbers of these animals. No true sportsman would jack animals or take fish over the limits.

Other kinds of behavior may not be illegal but are

clearly unacceptable. Cheating at card games, for instance, is outside the bounds of good sportsmanship. Cheating at any game, no matter how harmless, is uncceptable for everyone.

Accepting a bribe to "throw" an event is both unacceptable and illegal. We can't have athletic contests if gamblers or others are allowed to "fix" the results. The professional wrestling that is now so popular is more like a stage show than a real contest. There may be some horse races and some boxing matches that are "fixed." But in general, modern sports are free of fixes.

The most famous fix in American sports history involved the World Series in 1919. Many articles and books have been written about this event. In 1988, a movie was made about it called *Eight Men Out.* The Chicago White Sox were involved in this shameful incident. It is known as the Black Sox Scandal. Because it involved America's national pastime, the Black Sox Scandal is still talked about today.

The American League champion White Sox were heavily favored to beat the Cincinnati Reds that year. The White Sox had a better team. Naturally most bettors put their money on the White Sox. Gamblers began to bet a lot of money on the Reds. That made some people wonder what was going on. But the Series proceeded as scheduled. The Reds won.

Many months later, the story came out. Eight of the White Sox players were accused of dealing with gamblers. They were charged with "fixing" the Series. A court trial was held in 1921. By that time, much of the evidence had been "lost." None of the eight men were found guilty.

The court trial found these men innocent. But public opinion was against them. Many people feel that baseball is a special part of American life. It has to be totally honest. Its players must all set a good example for young people. The Commissioner of Baseball had the power to take any action he felt necessary. He barred all eight men from organized baseball for the rest of their lives. They could never play the game again.

Some people felt that punishment was too harsh. Some of the eight players had not done anything to help lose any of the games. They only talked about accepting money to fix the Series. But the future of baseball and all professional sports in the United States was at stake. A very clear line between acceptable and unacceptable conduct had to be set.

People who bet on sporting events often bet on more than who wins or loses. They bet on how many points a team will win by. What counts is the "point spread," the difference between the scores of the teams.

There have been several scandals over the years involving college basketball players. One took place in the

1984-85 season, with the players for Tulane University. In another case there were players for Boston College, in the 1978-79 season.

Gamblers paid these young basketball players to "shave points." Their teams could win, but by fewer points than was expected. The young men felt that no one was going to be hurt by their actions. Their school's team could win these games. The team would keep its standing in the league. They could even come out as champions at the end of the season. They just would not win certain games by as many points as was expected. Who would be the loser?

Well, there are several losers. People who bet on teams lost money to dishonest gamblers. All the honest players and their fans lost heart when they learned those games had been fixed. The sport of college basketball lost its reputation for honesty. When found guilty, the young men were expelled. They lost their chance of a college degree. They lost the chance to play basketball. Some of them spent time in jail. Most important of all, these young men lost their self respect.

Illegal conduct, of course, is more serious than unsportsmanlike conduct. People don't have to go to prison for showing bad sportsmanship. But whether they have committed a crime or an unsportsmanlike action, people have to go on living with themselves.

GETTING PHYSICAL

USING ILLEGAL DRUGS IS A CRIME. Accepting money to fix a game is a crime. People who do these things are punished in the real world. Athletic contests are played inside an imaginary circle. Inside this circle are the rules. When players break the rules, they or their team are usually just given a penalty. Then the game goes on as though nothing happened.

But sometimes players do something so serious that they break the circle. Their actions push outside the bounds of the game into the real world. This happens, for instance, when players attack an opponent on purpose and cause a physical injury. There have been cases where athletes have been very badly injured. Legal actions were taken against the players who made the attacks. This has happened in recent years with hockey players.

A player may feel he is being picked on by an opponent. He may be allowed to defend himself by responding. But he is not supposed to engage in physical violence. That goes outside the circle of the rules of the game.

Physical violence can be seen at almost any hockey game.

A certain amount of physical contact goes on within many sports. When does contact break the rules and when is it just poor sportsmanship?

In basketball, for instance, pushing an elbow into someone's face is a foul. It violates the rules of the game. It violates the code of sportsmanship. It can cause a serious injury. Grabbing a football player by the helmet

guard is also unacceptable. A man can have his neck
broken that way.

The most extreme cases of physical contact are probably those in ice hockey. Physical violence can be seen at
almost any hockey game. Players crash opponents
against the boards, or they slam into other players. These
actions can lead to fights. Then players swing and punch
and wrestle. This violence seems to be an accepted part
of the game today. Few hockey fans regard these fights
as displays of poor sportsmanship. Some people even
seem to enjoy this part of the game.

A player who uses a hockey stick to hurt an opponent
on purpose can cause real harm. Tripping a fast-skating
player on purpose calls for a penalty. So does "highstick-
ing." In this foul move, a player raises his stick up high
to hit an opponent in the face.

In many sports, the line between acceptable physical
attacks and illegal attacks is sometimes hard to see. In
football, linemen are praised for "blitzing" (stopping the
offense). And "sacking" the quarterback (knocking him to
the ground) is a key play. But defensive players will be
penalized if it looks like they have dumped a quarterback
after he has released the ball. This decision is left to the
referees. In most contests, referees must make decisions
without the benefit of "instant replay." Television cameras

catch each play in detail. It is often easier for fans at home to decide than it is for the officials.

There are some in-between cases. It is sometimes hard to know when football players have "piled on." Piling on is jumping onto a downed player. Sometimes the linemen simply can't stop their forward rush. Other times, though, players try to put a player out of the game.

Most players insist that they do not want to hurt any opponent personally. But they certainly don't mind seeing the star players being removed from the game. That way their own team gains an advantage. Where do you think the line of good sportsmanship is in a case like this?

There are some fuzzy areas in this matter of physical contact and sportsmanship. There are choices that are not just pure good or bad sportsmanship. Accidents can happen when people play a game too hard. Incidents happen because people take things too seriously. In sports such as boxing, football, or hockey, it often seems certain that someone will get hurt. Sometimes the injuries are serious.

You must decide for yourself if such dangerous sports are your game. But physical contact is no excuse for poor sportsmanship. Rough or tough as any sport may be, people can still play by all the rules. They can still show good sportsmanship.

7

BEYOND THE RULES

By now, several things about sportsmanship should be clear. Sportsmanship has to do with the rules of sports. But it is not only the rules. Sportsmanship often has to do with events just outside the areas of strict rules and penalties. The real world and sports both have their laws and rules. Good sportsmanship is what happens past these rules.

Strictly obeying the rules can sometimes seem like poor sportsmanship. Sometimes a coach or manager insists on enforcing a rule to gain an advantage or to restrict an opponent. It is hard to object to this practice, especially if a game is close. The coach has this right. But don't we all feel a bit ashamed, even when it is for our own team? It is embarrassing to win a game by the use of a minor rule.

There was a dramatic case like this in the 1988 Olympics. The USA women's gymnastic team was in a tight race for the bronze medal. The women's team from East Germany had a very close score. Only a fraction of a point separated the two teams. One of the members of the US team stood a few inches on the wrong side of a line while her teammate competed. The East German judge saw this. She insisted on enforcing a rule that penalized the US team. The American girl standing in the area had absolutely no effect on her teammate's performance. If the US team had not been penalized, it would have taken the bronze medal. Instead, the East German team won it. The East German judge's only comment was, "A regulation is a regulation." She was right, strictly speaking.

But don't most people feel that this is poor sportsmanship? Most people feel that it is better for everyone if we pay more attention to the true *spirit* of the rules of this world. This is part of true sportsmanship.

It must work both ways, however. It does no good to bend the rules only when you profit from it. That is *not* good sportsmanship. Each side must be willing to bend the rules a bit now and again. That will preserve the true spirit of the game.

Sportsmanship is something beyond the rules of the game. Two racers come to the end of a long, hard race. They are so close that they hold hands and go over the finish line together. That's true sportsmanship. Yes, it happens once in a while in a marathon or a bicycle race.

An individual or a team sees one of the competitors in serious trouble. He or she stops to help the other person or team. That is true sportsmanship. Something like this happens occasionally in a boat race or a dogsled race. If those in trouble were left behind, their lives might be in danger. So their opponents sacrifice their chances of winning. Going to the aid of those in trouble is more important. Next time they could be the ones who need help.

Some people think that professional athletes may have lost the sense of sportsmanship. After all, what they do is a job. But professional athletes often show sportsmanship. Look carefully at some of the major events—basketball and football in particular. Professional athletes often help their opponents up from the floor or ground. They often give each other a pat of approval. They congratulate each other after hard-played games. Watch the end of a boxing match. You may see the boxers hug each other. This is a sign of appreciation from one professional to another.

This kind of sportsmanship and respect is quite common in professional sports. On April 8, 1974, Hank Aaron hit his 715th home run. Someone had finally broken Babe Ruth's record. As Hank ran around the bases, some members of the opposing team, the Los Angeles Dodgers, gave him a high five. This gesture wasn't required by the rulebook. It was inspired by professional sportsmanship.

At some English soccer games, fans have been crushed in the crowd.

8

THE HUMAN CHOICE

SPORTSMANSHIP IS MADE UP OF A LOT OF DIFFERENT THINGS. Good sportsmanship sometimes overlaps into poor sportsmanship. Sportsmanship goes into other areas of life.

That is what makes sportsmanship valuable in our society. We take it for granted. But the ideal of good sportsmanship is not found in every society. Even in our own, it is quite a new idea. Our modern idea about sportsmanship appeared less than 100 years ago. Before that, the word referred only to physical skill in sports.

Good sportsmanship represents a more human, more relaxed way of life. Our society has strict laws that we must obey. Religions demand that people live up to various commandments. Most organizations and institutions demand that people observe their rules and regulations. Sportsmanship belongs to the part of life outside the strict rules. It is found in the spirit of things.

Good sportsmanship is even forgiving when it comes to poor sportsmanship. That's what makes good sports-

49

manship so special. The whole point is to be more understanding, more tolerant, more forgiving.

If you do exhibit poor sportsmanship sometime, it's not the end of the world. Everyone is human. We all make mistakes. The sign of a good sportsman is to forgive a poor sportsman, to give everyone a second chance.

Here is an example. Dave Winfield is known for his good sportsmanship on and off the field. He is a dedicated professional ballplayer. He gives some of his time and money to good causes. But Winfield is only human. Sometimes the pressure gets to him.

In 1984, Winfield came into the last game of the season in a race to win the American League batting championship. He was neck-and-neck with his teammate, Don Mattingly. Either one could win the crown. It depended on how well they hit in the last game. Mattingly got more hits than Winfield in that last game. He won the championship with .343. Winfield ended up with .340. After the game, the reporters expected to discuss all this with Winfield. He is known for being available to the press. But on that day, Winfield was upset at the way things had gone. He refused to meet the press. Many people felt that this was poor sportsmanship. Perhaps it was.

But most people would also agree that this one little episode doesn't make Dave Winfield a poor sportsman. Once in awhile, everyone makes a mistake. Good sports-

"Winning isn't everything, it's the only thing."
–Vince Lombardi

---

manship allows us to give people a second chance.

So sportsmanship is fairly complicated. It certainly goes far beyond the basketball courts and the law courts. It affects a lot more than athletes and sports.

How do you learn good sportsmanship? One way is in the selection of role models. You can find models of poor sportsmanship as well as models of good sportsmanship. They are all around us.

One issue of *Sports Illustrated* (April 24, 1988) featured a cover article about Tony Mandarich. He is an offensive lineman who was drafted in the first round by the Green Bay Packers in 1989. The magazine quoted Mandarich. "I came out for the coin toss. And even before the ref could flip the coin, I told Dave Haight, their noseguard, 'You're going to freaking die today!' I don't shake hands or anything. The ref turned his head and walked away."

Mandarich is doing a certain amount of boasting when he talks like that. It is part of a big linemen's job to try to frighten the opposition. So maybe he was putting on an act when he did that at the game. And maybe he talked like that to a reporter on purpose. But the article goes on to tell another story. During the game, Mandarich was filmed "sticking his hand inside the face mask of linebacker Jim Reilly and then nearly breaking him in half."

Does this mean that he is a poor sportsman? Not necessarily. Professional football players are expected to talk

and act tough. This kind of talk and behavior gets a lot
of publicity these days. After all, Tony Mandarich was on
the cover of that issue.

In the same issue, there is an article about another
young athlete. Kevin Johnson was then a fairly new
guard for the Phoenix Suns. His story is about a young
man's fine actions off the basketball court. Johnson gives
money to strangers in need. He gives away tickets to the
Suns games.

In one game a ball went out of bounds when Johnson
was standing close to it. The referee didn't see who
touched it last, so he asked Kevin. "I did," Kevin admitted. His coach may not have been very happy, but that is
what good sportsmanship is all about. It's easy to be a
good sportsman when you gain by it. The test comes
when you stand to lose from an act of good sportsmanship.

Does this kind of sportsmanship mean that Kevin
Johnson is less of an athlete than Tony Mandarich? Not so
far. Many other coaches praised this young NBA player.
The Knicks' coach calls Johnson "the toughest player
we've played in two years." Another tough and great
player, Charles Barkley, says Johnson "might be the best
pure point guard in basketball."

So you can be both a strong athlete and a good sportsman. You can even go with Vince Lombardi's idea that
"winning is the only thing" and still be a good sportsman.

"Nice guys finish last!"
–Leo Durocher

Sportsmanship is one of those qualities we choose for ourselves. Many values are demanded by society. Honesty is required by our society. Courage is often demanded. But sportsmanship is something we chose to value.

The dictionary helped us at the start of our search to understand sportsmanship. Then we had to see the word in action. We had to look at real life situations. But sooner or later, we have to leave the clear definitions behind. The boundaries in real life aren't always completely clear. When the clear definitions fade, we have to look in ourselves, not in a dictionary.

In the end, we do not find sportsmanship in the rule books, either. We must draw on our priorities, our values. "Sportsmanship" may be a new word and a new concept. But behind sportsmanship there are age-old values. Playing the game fair and square is what counts. Doing the best you can do is what counts.

Always doing their best allows professional athletes to retire with their self-respect. That is what lets all people look back on any experience with satisfaction. It is not a question of being "Number One." What really matters is that you practiced good sportsmanship.

Good sportsmanship can be demonstrated off the field by showing courtesy to others.

9

OFF THE FIELD

THERE ARE MANY WAYS GOOD SPORTSMANSHIP can be applied off the playing field. Good sportsmanship is part of our society. The language is part of our culture. The ideal shows up in many activities.

Jack Kemp, Secretary of Housing and Urban Development under President George Bush, had been a presidential candidate. A magazine article explained why Kemp failed in the race for the Republican Party's presidential nomination in 1988. "Kemp...could not persuade himself...to violate the rules of sportsmanship. He could not say bad things about his opponents, no matter how often his handlers pleaded with him to do so."

The use of the word "handlers" is interesting. It compares the presidential candidates to boxers or race horses. This supports the idea of politics as an athletic contest. (It is no coincidence that Jack Kemp was once quarterback of the Buffalo Bills.) By saying Kemp wouldn't "violate the rules of sportsmanship," the writer is sure we all know what these are. He then is sure that these rules hold true in the world outside gyms and playing fields. He also is

Chapter Nine

sure that they are high standards. He is sure they are higher than the standards followed by some presidential candidates.

Sportsmanship is an ideal that can exist outside sports itself. It applies to many areas of our lives. Consider all the other competitions that you go through in your schooling. There is competition to do well in classes and get good grades. There is competition to get leading roles in plays or to sing solos in musical events. There may be a competition to win an elective office or some award.

Many of the things we said about athletes and organized sports are present in such competitions. Determination, dedication, training, pressures from family and other adults to succeed are involved. You can cheat at tests just as some gamblers cheat at cards. You can resort to drugs just as some adults do. You can bend the rules until you have broken them, just as some athletes do. But you will do better if you follow the ideals of good sportsmanship.

To do things right or to get along well with other people, don't we have to practice good sportsmanship? We want to try for the best in everything we do. But we do not want to succeed at the price of stepping on others. When we win, we should not rub it in. When we lose out, we should accept it well. This is as true in your personal life as it is on the playing field.

We might even say that sportsmanship could guide us in almost all our activities and relationships. If you just want to play by the rules and not think about the spirit of sportmanship, you can get by in this world. But it wouldn't be a very pleasant or smooth-running world if everyone insisted on that. This is as true with driving a car as with promoting world peace. Traffic keeps flowing smoothest and safest when everyone practices good sportsmanship behind the wheel. And countries would get on better if they paid less attention to legal treaties and more to the spirit of good sportsmanship.

It is the extra efforts that result in good relations. You get nowhere if you always insist on imposing rules or on getting everything you have a right to. Cooperation is basically good sportsmanship. Consideration of other people and their rights is also good sportsmanship. These are ideals to live by. They make all our lives richer and more worthwhile.

Glossary: *Explaining New Words*

amateur A nonprofessional. Amateur sports are played for the love of the game, not for money.

anabolic steroid Manufactured chemicals made to increase such masculine characteristics as muscular size and bodily strength. They can have a bad effect on other bodily parts and functions.

blitz In football, a play in which more than the usual number of defensive players quickly rush in to catch the offensive backfield off guard.

drug A chemical that affects the body's processes. When prescribed by a doctor, it is a medicine. The term "drug" now usually refers to those chemicals used by people to obtain some special sensation without any medical prescription.

enhance To increase or improve. An enhancement drug improves some natural ability or characteristic, as a drug taken to build up muscles.

fix To try to control the outcome of a game or contest by bribery or another improper method.

foul A move or play outside the rules of a game.

highstick To carry a hockey stick at an illegal height so as to put an opposing player in danger.

hypertension High blood pressure. It can come from natural causes or from drugs.

ideal The thought of something that is held as a goal we might try to attain. A standard of excellence.

jack To hunt or fish at night by shining a light into the face of an animal so that it is confused and stays still.

Olympic ideal The Olympic Games were founded by the ancient Greeks in 776 BC as a series of athletic and other events to which all Greek city-states were invited to send contestants. The games were held every four years at the shrine of the god Zeus at Olympia. They were stopped in the year AD 394. The modern Olympic Games were started again in 1896 and were supposed to uphold what are thought to be the ideal goals of the Olympics: only the pleasure of participation and the spirit of coop-eration between countries.

prescription A written direction given by a doctor to a druggist to prepare and sell special medicine.

priority Something we think is more important than other things.

recreational drugs Drugs taken just for pleasure of the moment and not for any medical reason.

recruit To look for athletes and persuade them to come to a particular school or join a team.

sack A football term. A defensive player or players

tackle the quarterback behind the line of scrimmage before the quarterback can pass or get rid of the ball. The term comes from the ancient practice of placing a person in a sack and drowning him.

shave points In sporting contests, to deliberately make fewer points than might be possible. Usually done in order to fall below the point spread agreed upon by bettors on the game.

sportsmanship Conduct associated with a good athlete and involving fair and honest rivalry. Good manners at all levels. Accepting winning or losing with good humor.

stimulant Anything that increases the regular activity of some part of the body for the moment.

standard Something that has been set up by tradition or general agreement as an example to be followed.

throw (a contest) In sports, when one contestant or team deliberately does less than they are able to, in order to lose. Usually it is done for money or to satisfy professional gamblers.

testosterone A male hormone. It is a chemical compound that provides certain characteristics in males' bodily features and processes.

value: Something that has its own worth and is regarded as holding a high place in our own or society's scale of priorities.

For Further Reading

Etter, Les. *Get Those Rebounds!.* New York: Hastings House, 1978. One of many fine sports novels for young people that stress the elements of good sportsmanship. This one is about an African-American boy whose brother plays for the Los Angeles Lakers. It deals with his struggle to escape from his brother's reputation and find his own identity.

Harrison, Marta, and the Non-Violence and Children Program. *For the Fun of It: Selected Cooperative Games for Children and Adults.* Philadelphia: Friends of Peace Committee, 1975. One of many books now available that promote new games that stress cooperation and eliminate physical violence.

Lipsyte, Robert. *The Contender.* New York: Harper and Row, 1967. Although written over 20 years ago, this is still one of the better youth novels about sports. It tells the story of a 17-year-old African-American who begins to train to be a professional boxer. It conveys the many pressures and problems that confront such a young American to this day.

Liston, Robert. *The Great Teams: Why They Win All the Time.* New York: Doubleday & Co., 1979. An examination of some of the teams with the best winning records that reveals what they have in common.

Among other things, they have a shared sense of team spirit that has more to do with good sportsmanship than just technical skills.

Sports Illustrated. New York City. This magazine, published weekly, is perhaps the most available and most readable account of all aspects of current athletics and sports. As such, it is the best record of both good and bad sportsmanship in those fields these days.

Stanbler, Irwin. *Women in Sports.* New York: Doubleday & Co., 1975. A series of biographies of famous American women athletes that provides many illustrations of both good and bad sportsmanship.

Telander, Rick. *Heaven Is a Playground.* New York: Simon & Schuster, 1976. This book describes the game of basketball as played by young African-Americans during the summer at a New York City playground. Although it may not discuss sportsmanship as such, it ends up having a lot to say about the subject.

Winfield, Dave. *A Player's Life.* New York: W.W. Norton & Co., 1988. Without preaching about good or bad sportsmanship, this frank autobiography reveals a lot about how someone can strive to be both an outstanding athlete and a fine human being in today's world.

INDEX

Index

About the Author

John Bowman is the author of numerous books for young people.He has also written several histories of baseball, including his latest, *Diamonds in the Rough.*

Photo Credits and Acknowledgments

Cover Photo: Charles Waldron
Pages 2,10,13,17,20,22-23,28,34,54, Charles Waldron; p.24,30,32,48, Wide World Photos;
pg.36, The Bettman Archive; pg. 43, FPG International/ Howard Zryb

Design and Production: Blackbirch Graphics,Inc.

DATE DUE

19035

175   Bowman, John.
BOW   Sportsmanship